The MacDougall Twins
With
Sherlock Holmes

Book #2:
Attack of the Violet
Vampire

Paperback ISBN 9781780927671
ePub ISBN 978-1-78092-768-8
PDF ISBN 978-1-78092-769-5

Published in the UK by MX Publishing
335 Princess Park Manor, Royal Drive, London, N11 3GX
www.mxpublishing.co.uk

Cover Illustration by Brian Belanger
Cover Compilation by www.staunch.com

<u>Dedication</u>

<u>Derrick's Dedication</u>

For Phoebe -

A girl as sharp as Sherlock Holmes, as playful as Toby, and as adventurous as the MacDougall Twins

<u>Brian's Dedication</u>

To Gram -

(Barbara Rousseau to most of you)

For teaching me how to be young

Table of Contents

Chapter 1: Sherlock Holmes's Special Guests

"This is so exciting," said Mrs. MacDougall. "I've never ridden in a **landau**[1] carriage before." The MacDougall family was

---

[1] **Fun Fact:** A landau is a carriage that is convertible, meaning that its top can be removed. It was very expensive to own, or even to ride in a landau, which is why it is such a treat for the MacDougall family.

riding in a luxury carriage to go to the theatre. Tonight was the first performance of a play based on a Sherlock Holmes case.

"I just hope the play isn't boring," said Mr. MacDougall. "Dressing in a suit! Riding in a gold plated coach! This ain't to my liking," he complained. Mr. MacDougall was a chimney sweep. He preferred wearing dirty jeans rather than a fancy suit.

"No need to worry, Father," said Emma MacDougall. "This is a play about Sherlock Holmes, the world's greatest detective."

"And," Jimmy, Emma's twin brother added, "it deals with a giant killer snake!"

"Aww, that sounds good," Mr. MacDougall chuckled, "but does it have a Violet Vampire?!?"

"Oh Dad, not that again!" said the twins together. Jimmy and Emma MacDougall were ten year old twin detectives. They had solved The Case of the Mysterious Airship. Now, all the children of London came to them for help. Since the airship mystery, Jimmy and Emma had been working nonstop. They helped their friend, Nolan the Newsboy, find his stolen stack of papers. They helped the pet store solve the case of the kidnapped kitten. They even helped **Scotland Yard** [2]track down a missing little boy, who was really a foreign prince.

"Dad, everyone knows that there is no such thing as a vampire," Emma scolded.

Mr. MacDougall smiled at his fiery, red-haired daughter. "How do you know? It's in all the papers."

Emma shook her head. There had been odd reports in East London of a bat-winged monster attacking people. At first, it was one or two reports. Now, it seemed like every other day, people were reporting seeing a strange, violet colored creature with sharp teeth, and glowing red eyes.

---

[2] **Fun Fact:** Scotland Yard is not a yard, and it is not in Scotland!! Scotland Yard is the name of the Metropolitan Police Force, the police that patrol most of London.

"We'll see if someone brings us the case," laughed Jimmy. "Tonight, let's just enjoy the show."

With all of the excitement in their lives, Jimmy and Emma were looking forward to a night at the theatre. Sherlock Holmes had invited the MacDougall family as his special guests. He knew that the family, especially Mrs. MacDougall, would love a grand night out.

Mrs. MacDougall jumped for joy when they received the invitation. She wore her best dress that evening, a blue silk dress. She also wore the MacDougall diamond ring. This ring had been in the MacDougall family for over 1,000 years. At one time, it was worn by the Queen of Scotland! Mrs. MacDougall rarely wore the ring. She was afraid it might get lost or stolen.

The landau carriage pulled up in front of the Adelphi Theatre. The four horses whinnied, and the driver got down to open the door. Mrs. MacDougall and Emma were the first ones out of the carriage, followed by Mr. MacDougall, and then Jimmy.

"Oww," yelped Jimmy. He had bonked his head on the top of the carriage door. Jimmy was very tall for his age. He often went in disguise as an adult.

"Are you all right?" asked Mrs. MacDougall.

"Of course," answered Jimmy, rubbing the back of his head. "Now, let's go see Sherlock Holmes. I'm looking forward to a fun night!"

Little did Jimmy know that far above him, on the theatre roof, a dark form, with glowing red eyes, watched the MacDougall family. The vampire smiled, revealing its sharp fangs. It chuckled in a deep, scary tone. The creature unfolded its massive wings, let out a howl, and prepared to attack.

Chapter 2: The Vampire Attacks!

When the MacDougall family saw the line to get into the Adelphi Theatre, they couldn't believe their eyes. The line was so long that it went from the theatre[3] entrance out to the street; then, it curved around to the right of the building, and must have gone on for close to a half of a mile.

"It looks like Mr. Holmes's play is a huge hit," said Mrs. MacDougall happily.

"Unfortunately, he must not be here yet," Emma stated, pointing to the long line. "They want Sherlock to be the first one inside, since he is the Guest of Honor."

"'Well, let's go to the front," said Mr. MacDougall. "There's no reason for us to wait in that line, seeing as we're the guests of honor."

---

[3] **Fun Fact:** Theatre or theater? In 1897, when this story takes place, the spelling "theatre" was more common. Today, the spelling "theater" is mainly used. Both spellings are considered correct.

"Actually, Dad," Jimmy explained. "Sherlock Holmes is the guest of honor. We are his guests."

"Guests of honor, or guests of the guests, what difference does that make?" Mr. MacDougall asked, getting flustered.

"It means that we have to stand in the back of the line," Emma said, pointing to the queue, which was getting longer and longer.

"Come on, Nedley," Mrs. MacDougall said to her husband, amusingly. "You'll still get to sit with Dr. Watson."

As the family walked to the end of the queue, Mr. MacDougall complained loudly, "What's the point of being guests of the guests if you got to wait in a long line?!?"

When they finally reached the rear of the line, Jimmy and Emma were surprised to see their good friend, Nolan the Newsboy. He was not wearing his usual patched up clothes, but instead was dressed as a gentleman. His hair was slicked back. He had on a dark suit with a white bow tie.

"Nolan, you look great," said Jimmy, who was shocked to see such a change in his friend's appearance.

"Hi Emma and Jimmy," said Nolan, happy to see his two friends. "I knew you two would be here, with the play about Sherlock Holmes and what not. Gotta take in the culture, I always say."

"You come to the theatre often?" Jimmy asked, surprised.

"'Course, my friend. I may be a newsboy, but I got class. I go to all the great shows. You know, the ones with the cowboys and gangsters and the like. If I can't see the world, I might as well see it in the theatre, I always..."

"Always what, Nolan?" Emma asked. But Nolan didn't respond. He was staring up into the sky. His face had gone pale and turned slightly green. Nolan's knees were shaking and his body broke out in a cold sweat.

Jimmy and Emma turned to see what had scared Nolan so much. There, in the sky, was a massive monster. It had giant dragon-like wings, sharp claws, and glowing red eyes. Its skin color was a dark, violet tone. The creature looked like a gargoyle, as if a stone creature from an ancient church cathedral had come to life.

Suddenly, there was a mass panic as the vampire swooped down towards the street, towards the people waiting to get into the theatre. Everyone screamed and scattered. Some people knocked and banged on the theatre door to try to get in; others ran out into the busy street traffic. The **hansoms**, **carriages**, and buses[4] in the street tried to stop their horses. Many crashed into each other. Horses whinnied and screeched. Fortunately, no one was hurt.

"We have to get Mom and Dad out of here," Jimmy said, as his parents looked around bewildered at the situation. "Emma, where are you going?"

Jimmy called out as Emma ran right into the traffic. Jimmy couldn't figure out what his sister was doing. Then he saw. In the middle of the street was a mother with a baby in a pram[5]. She was just standing there, terrified, and the vampire was heading straight for her.

Emma got to the mother just as the vampire was about to grab her. Emma, with all her might, shoved the mother and the baby out

---

[4] **Fun Fact:** In 1897, the main form of transportation in London was horse-drawn carriages. There are a number of different types, such as hansoms, omnibuses, and growlers. See the first MacDougall Twins mystery, *The Amazing Airship Adventure*, for more information.

[5] **Fun Fact:** Pram or stroller? It depends on if you are speaking British or American English. In Britain, the term pram is more common than stroller. In America, the opposite is true.

of the way. She felt the wing of the vampire swoosh just above her head, and she heard the vampire give a deep, booming chuckle.

"Flee you fools! Flee!" the vampire called out as everyone continued dashing away from the creature.

Then, it was over. The vampire disappeared. The crowd had dispersed, and all that was left were the broken carriages in the middle of the street, a few horses that were still kicking and running wild; Emma, who was heading back to her family, and the other three MacDougall family members, all huddled together by the side of the Adelphi Theatre.

"Wow!" Mr. MacDougall called out. He sounded more impressed than scared. "There really is a Violet Vampire! What do you think about that?"

Jimmy and Emma were about to respond when their mother called out. "Oh no! OH NO!!"

"Mother, what's wrong? Are you hurt?" Emma asked.

"It's my ring! My family ring! IT'S GONE!!"

Chapter 3: A New Monster?

They searched everywhere for Mrs. MacDougall's ring. Emma crawled on the sidewalk, lifting every scrap of paper, every leaf, and every piece of trash to see if her mother's ring had fallen to the ground. Jimmy scanned the street, prying up every loose cobblestone, just to make certain that the family heirloom hadn't, somehow, fallen underneath. Mrs. MacDougall double checked and triple checked her purse. Even Mr. MacDougall checked his pockets to see if the ring could have fallen into his clothes.

As the family searched for the ring, police officers arrived outside the theatre to help clean up the carriage wrecks in the street. They were also looking for clues about the Violet Vampire. Nolan asked a few police officers if they could help find Mrs. MacDougall's ring, but they were too busy. They didn't have time to look for a lost ring when a vampire was loose in the city.

After their frantic search, Jimmy and Emma returned to their parents empty handed. No one found any sign of the ring. The family was about to give up hope when they heard a voice say, "Why, bless my soul, if it isn't the famous Baker Street Youth Detectives."

The MacDougalls all turned to see Nolan, smiling, and holding the hand of a police officer with a friendly, familiar face. He was lean, had dark eyes, and his thin, wiry moustache made his face look like that of a ferret, but his smile was contagious and gave the family hope.

"Inspector Lestrade!" Emma cried out joyfully. Then, she ran up to the officer and gave him a big hug. "We are so happy to see you."

"And it is a delight to see you as well, but from what this young gentleman says, it sounds like you've run into a bit of trouble," Lestrade surmised. "Now, let's have the story from the beginning."

Mrs. MacDougall explained how her ring went missing. She described every aspect of her family ring, and Lestrade took detailed notes. Finally, the inspector said, "We will keep our eyes out for your ring, but first we've got a monster to catch!"

"A monster?!?" the twins shouted together.

"Of course. Everyone knows that there is no such thing as a vampire," Lestrade lectured. "However, we are finding new species every day, like the Yeti or that dinosaur living in Loch Ness. Yes, yes, all we need is to catch the Violet Vampire, and Scotland Yard will be famous. Maybe they'll even name the creature after me. Can't you see it? *The Flying Lestrade!*"

"That's...an interesting idea," said Emma, gritting her teeth. She was too polite to tell Inspector Lestrade what she really thought of his theory.

"What does Sherlock Holmes think of your monster idea?" asked Jimmy, trying not to chuckle.

"Oh, I haven't had a chance to tell Mr. Holmes, but I hope to speak with him later this evening. He's been too busy, pursuing Jeb Peterson and his gang. They are a gang of outlaws from America who have been committing robberies across Britain."

"Peterson gang?" Mr. MacDougall puzzled, "Never heard of no Peterson gang."

"They go by many names, Nedley. Their leader is sometimes called Will Mackenty, sometimes David Marcum, but, for now, goes by Jeb Peterson. No matter what name he goes by, it is always spelled 'trouble'."

"That explains why Sherlock Holmes wasn't at the theatre tonight," Nolan concluded. "Too busy chasing the crooks."

"While Mr. Holmes is tracking that Peterson gang," Inspector Lestrade smirked, "I'll get me a Violet Vampire. Say, Jimmy and

Emma, why don't you help out? Scotland Yard would love to work with the MacDougall Twins."

"Of course, Mr. Lestrade, they'll be more than happy to help," Mr. MacDougall proudly stated. "That's why they're called the Baker Street Youth Detectives."

"They may help," Mrs. MacDougall interrupted. She spoke sternly. "However, they must first complete their schooling for the day. Only after their lessons may they go out to help. The Violet Vampire is important, but nothing is as important as my children getting a good education."

"Of course, Frances," Inspector Lestrade reassured Mrs. MacDougall. "The children's schooling is priority number one. I'll stop in tomorrow afternoon. Emma, I'd love having your assistance interviewing witnesses. Now, I'll have a few of my policemen look for your ring." Inspector Lestrade was interrupted by a loud rumble of thunder. "Let's get your family home," he said, looking up at the dark clouds in the sky. "It looks like it is going to rain."

A **police wagon**[6] came to take the MacDougall family home. They said goodbye to Nolan and to Inspector Lestrade. Then, they entered the battered wagon and began their journey back to 222 Baker Street. In the wagon, everyone sat quietly. It had been an exciting night. Jimmy wondered what the Violet Vampire could be. Could it be an unknown animal, like Inspector Lestrade thought? Could it somehow be a person in disguise? Or could it be a real life vampire?

---

[6] **Fun Fact:** A police wagon, also known as patrol wagon, paddy wagon, and Black Maria, is a police vehicle used to hold and transport prisoners. In 1897, the police wagon was a horse drawn carriage which contained a locking cell.

Chapter 4: A Secret Message

"MONSTER MENACE! THE VIOLET VAMPIRE STRIKES AGAIN!" screamed the headline of the morning's newspaper. The MacDougall family was having breakfast and Mr. MacDougall, Jimmy, and Emma were taking turns reading over the front page story of the vampire's rampage outside the Adelphi Theatre.

"That's quite a story. Too bad I'm off to work. I'd like to see you two catch that vampire," Mr. MacDougall winked and beamed. "Don't you want to read the story, dear?" he asked Mrs. MacDougall.

"No, no..." Mrs. MacDougall responded while scanning the back of the newspaper. "I'm reading the announcements to see if anyone found my ring."

"We can go look, Mom," Emma said.

"Yes, we might have more luck in the daylight," Jimmy stated excitedly. He was hoping to get back on the case and not have to worry about school.

"After you are done your lessons for the day," Mrs. MacDougall sternly reminded her children while she buttered a piece of toast. "Inspector Lestrade fully agreed with me on that point."

"Yes, Mom," Emma agreed. "He won't be sending a coach to get us until this afternoon, but we can spend some time looking then."

"The afternoon can't come soon enough," Jimmy muttered. He didn't like studying from books. Jimmy much preferred solving a crime rather than solving an algebra problem.

Mr. MacDougall got up from the dining room table. "Well, I will see you all this evening. Got a full day of work ahead of me," the jolly father said as he cleared his dishes and headed out the door. He stepped outside, paused, and then asked, "Hey Jimmy, could you help me with my brooms, please?"

Jimmy was baffled. He got up from the table and went outside to help his father. "I didn't think you had any brooms with you,' Jimmy said, confused.

Mr. MacDougall closed the door quickly to make sure they wouldn't be overheard. "I didn't want to upset your mom, but look what I found attached to the door this morning when I stepped out to get the paper." Mr. MacDougall held up a thin opened envelope. "I think you know who it's from," Mr. MacDougall chuckled. "Come on now, have a look."

Jimmy quickly unfolded the letter. His eyes ate every word written by his good friend Sherlock Holmes.

Dear James and Emma,

I do apologize in advance for my lack of assistance on the case of the Violet Vampire. As you know, I am currently indisposed. I must catch the Peterson gang before they strike again. Inspector Lestrade told me his theory of the Violet Vampire. It was utterly ridiculous, so I am glad that you will be assisting him, Emma. Jimmy, I would like you to look for your mother's ring. I am sending my most reliable and special agent to assist you. My fear is that the ring was stolen. We shall have our answers soon enough.

Take good care of yourselves. I will call upon you this evening.

Your dear friend,

Sherlock Holmes

"The ring was stolen? But, how?!?" Jimmy questioned aloud.

"I wondered that myself," Mr. MacDougall said quietly. "That's why I wanted you to read this note outside. I didn't want your mother alarmed. You share this with your sister and make sure your mother thinks her ring was lost. If she knows it's been stolen, she'll never let us go back to the theatre."

Jimmy grinned. "I didn't think you wanted to go to the theatre anyway."

"And miss out on Sherlock Holmes wrestling a snake? I wouldn't miss it for the world!"

Jimmy and his father burst out laughing, and then Jimmy asked his father, "Say, why did you open the letter if you knew it was addressed to Emma and me?"

"Your mom's not the only one who needs to look after you," Mr. McDougall admitted, and patted Jimmy on the back. "Now you go on back inside and get that reading and writing done. I expect a full report on your adventure when I get home from work."

"Finding a ring doesn't sound very exciting to me," Jimmy sadly admitted.

"Nonsense," Mr. MacDougall assured his son. "If Sherlock Holmes wants you looking for that ring, it's got to be about more than just the ring. Besides you get to work with his special agent...Oops! Look at the time! I gotta run Jimmy, but I'll see you at dinner." With that, Mr. MacDougall adjusted his hat, waved goodbye, and tramped off to work.

Jimmy went back inside the house, sat down at the dining table, and slipped his sister the letter from Sherlock Holmes. She gave him a funny look, and he nodded his head as if to say, *read it, but make sure Mom doesn't see.* Emma was smart enough to excuse herself from the table and go up to her room to get her school books. Jimmy knew she'd read the letter before she reached the door to her bedroom.

As he sat at the table, finishing his last sip of tomato juice, he wondered about the letter. Who was this special agent, and why did Jimmy need his help? He only needed to find a ring. Or did he? Was there more to it than that? In fact, the big question for Jimmy was how did the stolen ring connect with the Violet Vampire?

Could the Violet Vampire have taken the ring? That made no sense.

These questions kept running through Jimmy's mind, and he wondered how he'd be able to concentrate on his school work.

Chapter 5: Sherlock's Most Reliable and Special Agent

Jimmy kept re-reading the same paragraph of his history book over and over again. He tried to focus on the words about the Battle of Agincourt, but his mind kept drifting back to the letter from Sherlock Holmes. *Who was this most reliable and special agent?*

Finally, Jimmy closed the book and shook his head. He rubbed his eyes, got up, and stretched. He thought taking a moment to walk around the study would give his mind a little break. After that, he would be able to return to his history book and actually pay attention. Before wandering away, he looked over to his sister and could see she was working very hard. Emma was intently studying a book called *Rodent Biology*. She seemed to be devouring every word on the page. From the wry grin on her face, Jimmy knew she was on to something.

"You've made a discovery, haven't you?" Jimmy asked his sister.

"I have a theory, yes," Emma answered, snapping the book shut and taking a stretch break herself. "I need more data, more research, before I can say anything."

"Aww, you can tell me what you've figured out," Jimmy begged.

"No, not without more evidence. I don't want to put ideas in your mind, and then find out I was completely wrong later. It might throw you off of your search for the ring. Anyway, once I interview the other Violet Vampire witnesses, I'll be able to draw a conclusion and possibly solve the case."

"Why did I get stuck looking for a lousy ring?" Jimmy muttered.

"That ring is our family heirloom," Emma reminded Jimmy. "It is your piece of the mystery to solve. I know it isn't as action-packed as you like it to be. Just remember, it is very important to Mother. She is-" Emma was interrupted by a loud banging on the front door. "I bet that is Inspector Lestrade," Emma stated matter-of-factly, and dashed off to get the door.

Emma and her mother warmly greeted the inspector and one of his constables. "Are you ready to help solve the case?" Lestrade asked Emma.

"Of course," Emma proudly responded.

"And I understand Mr. Holmes has a different task for you, James?" Lestrade inquired.

"I guess so," Jimmy glumly answered. He had joined the group at the doorway hoping Lestrade would take him along with his sister.

"Well, no dawdling. We've got work ahead of us, Emma. We have to catch this new monster. Say, I believe this vampire may eat fish like that dinosaur in Loch Ness..."

Inspector Lestrade continued his theory about the vampire as Jimmy closed the door and let out a long sigh.

"I know looking for the family ring is not very exciting," Mrs. MacDougall said to her son. "It is very important to me, and I appreciate it." She gave Jimmy a kiss on his cheek and told him to go back to his studies.

Ten minutes later, there was another knock on the door. Jimmy sprinted from the study to the door while Mrs. MacDougall called after him, "No running in the house!" When

Jimmy reached the front door, he threw it open and was surprised to see someone he knew quite well. Standing in the doorway was Steven, the cab driver. The boy was standing tall and had a great grin on his face. Next to Steven was a mangy-looking mutt. The dog had

short gray hair, floppy ears, and looked like it desperately needed a bath. Jimmy could not tell the age of the canine. He thought the dog looked quite old, yet there was a youthful aura to the animal. It seemed almost like a wise and ancient puppy.

"Hello there Jimmy. It's always a pleasure to see you."

"Wow!" Jimmy exclaimed. "You had me fooled the whole time, Steven."

"What do you mean?" Steven asked while scratching his head.

"You are a secret agent to Sherlock Holmes!"

Steven's eyes got wide and his face dropped. Then, the boy burst out laughing. "Ha, ha, ha, that's a good one Jimmy. Me, a regular cab driver working for Sherlock Holmes. Maybe they'll call me the Baker Street Cabbie Detective. Ha, Ha, Ha!"

"What's all this ruckus?" Mrs. MacDougall interjected as she joined the two boys at the door.

"Sorry, ma'am," Steven said. "He thought I was a detective, and I couldn't help laughing."

Mrs. MacDougall glared. "Why did you think he was a detective, James?"

"Sorry Mom, but Sherlock Holmes told me he'd send someone to help me look for your ring."

"Did he, now," Mrs. MacDougall responded, and Jimmy was surprised to see his mother look relieved. "All that effort to help me look for my lost ring. Perhaps Mr. Holmes is a gentleman who deserves more credit than I give him. Well, where is this agent?"

"He's right here," Steven said and gestured down to the canine at his feet.

"You mean the dog?" Jimmy gasped.

Mrs. MacDougall furrowed her brow and pursed her lips. Her eyes turned to slits as she leaned forward to examine the mutt before her.

Jimmy was silent, afraid that if he said anything, his mother would explode like a stick of dynamite.

"By any chance is this dog's name Toby?" she gasped in a voice filled with awe.

"Yes, indeed, ma'am. I fetched him straight from Pinchin Lane, I did," Steven beamed with a Cheshire cat grin.

Jimmy was lost. He thought his mother would be furious. "The dog's a detective, and you're happy, Mom?"

"When you were a newborn baby, Jimmy, this dog helped Sherlock Holmes find a hidden treasure chest," Mrs. MacDougall explained to her son. "If he can find the famous Agra treasure, then I'm sure finding my lost ring will be no problem at all. Now, give me a moment and I'll fetch another piece of my jewelry." Mrs. MacDougall disappeared into the house.

Jimmy looked down at Toby, who was patiently waiting on the front step for Mrs. MacDougal to return. "You certainly are

Sherlock's most surprising agent. Can you really find my family ring?"

Steven slapped Jimmy on the back. "Just you wait and see, Jimmy. When your mom comes back with a piece of jewelry and Toby here gets her scent, there'll be no stopping him. I'll take you back to the Adelphi Theatre, and then you'll see this dog in action!"

Chapter 6: The Canine Conundrum

Steven steered his cab through the London traffic of omnibuses, growlers, and other cabs. Bess pulled the hansom along at a quick gallop. The horse was moving swiftly, but this was a much slower pace than the last time Jimmy was a passenger in Steven's cab. A few months ago, they had pursued the mad bomber. Bess had moved as fast as a lightning bolt then to catch the villain and his **cob horses**[7]. Now, Bess would get Jimmy to the Adelphi Theatre, but at a reasonable pace. No one would lose their hat in the breeze, and Jimmy wouldn't lose his lunch from motion sickness.

Jimmy was sitting in the carriage next to Toby. The dog was leaning his head out of the cab window. The way Toby looked at the London surroundings made Jimmy think of

---

[7] **Fun Fact:** There is no breed of horse known as a cob horse. A cob horse is a horse that is short and strong. These horses are excellent at pulling heavy carriages.

Sherlock Holmes. Mr. Holmes also had a similar look on his face when he was taking in information and going to his mind palace. Of course, Mr. Holmes didn't wag his tail, and when he looked out a window, he kept his tongue inside his mouth. Jimmy still wondered how this mutt was going to be the magical missing link to finding his mom's ring.

"Say, Steven," Jimmy called to his friend. "Is your boss okay with you having a dog in the car?"

"Why of course he is," Steven replied and swerved to miss a man who wandered out into the street. "Ole Bess here has pulled her share of critters. One time I had to pick up a baby seal from the Docks and bring it to the London Zoo, but at the same time, I had to get a bear cub for Buffalo Bill's Wild West Show. So there I was with a baby seal and a bear cub sharing me cab, sitting beside themselves. I thought they'd get into all sorts of mischief, maybe even a fight, but they had the best time. They just looked out the window and cooed. Course I don't count

Toby in the same league as show animals or zoo specimens. Why, Toby is practically human."

Bess came to a quick stop as Steven called, "Whoa!" Jimmy saw they had arrived back at the Adelphi Theatre. The building's arched entryway looked grander in the daylight.

Jimmy was impressed by the Grecian architecture with columns straight out of ancient Rome. Toby plopped down onto the street, called the Strand, and Jimmy followed. He made sure not to bump his head on the way out of the carriage.

"I'll be back in another hour or so," Steven called down from his carriage perch. "I bet you'll have your mum's ring by then. Maybe you'll even have the Violet Vampire in irons!"

Jimmy laughed and waved goodbye to his friend. Then he looked down at the big-eyed, mangy dog who was gazing up at him. "Alright Toby, let's see what you can do."

Reaching into his pocket, Jimmy removed a locket his mother had given him for Toby to get her scent. The dog held his nose over the locket in Jimmy's palm, took two sniffs, and then dashed down the street, avoiding puddles as he went. Jimmy chased after Toby, splashing through the puddles to keep up with the mutt. *How can an animal that old be that fast?* Jimmy wondered as he huffed along.

Just as quickly as Toby started, the animal suddenly stopped at a street corner where an omnibus without passengers was parked. The driver was standing on the corner, leaning against his vehicle while his horses ate some oats from a bag. The man had a swirling mustache and a **bowler**[8] on his head. Jimmy couldn't make out much more of him than that. The man was reading the newspaper, which was covering up the upper part of his body.

"Excuse me, sir," Jimmy said to the man. "But were you at the theatre last night when the Violet Vampire attacked?"

The man kept reading the paper, barely giving Jimmy any attention. Then he responded without looking up. "I don't work nights. That's Kelly's shift. But no, lad, I wasn't here."

---

[8] **Fun Fact:** A bowler is a type of hat also known as a billycock or derby. The hat is made of a hard felt and has a rounded crown. This was a common hat for workers to wear at the end of the 19th century.

"But Kelly was here?" Jimmy asked eagerly. He hoped he might actually have a lead.

The man lowered his paper. Jimmy thought he would look gruff at the questioning, but the man had a wry grin on his face. "Heh, sorry son, this bus was picking up passengers at the time of the attack. It was nowhere near the Strand nor the Adelphi. I'm sure you can find someone else who was here last night who can tell you stories about the attack. I'd be careful, though. The day after an event like that is when stories can become just that, stories, if you know what I mean?"

"Yes, sir," Jimmy agreed. He knew what the bus driver meant. When Emma and he interviewed witnesses, their stories changed over time. A witness who said that they saw a six foot tall burglar may change it to an eight foot tall burglar the next day. These were known as big fish tales. Jimmy knew that was why it was so important to interview witnesses soon after a crime, before their imagination ran wild.

"Now, lad, that man over there may have seen something...well, maybe not." The bus driver said indicating a man across the street.

Jimmy saw a blind beggar standing on the corner. He was a tall, balding, red-headed man dressed in rags and holding out a tin cup for donations. Jimmy knew he was blind from the thick, dark-lensed glasses he wore.

A banker approached the beggar, said a few words to him, and put some coins in his cup. Even across the street, Jimmy could hear the beggar blessing the man for his kindness. Jimmy looked down at Toby. The dog had given Jimmy a lead. Even with the ground still wet from the previous night's rain, the dog's nose had picked up the scent.

"Perhaps Mom's ring was taken by a person who was picked up by a coach, or carriage, or even a bus at the corner," Jimmy found himself saying to Toby. The dog just looked up at him, waiting for its next mission.

"Come along Toby," Jimmy called down, and the dog began wandering along. Jimmy hoped Toby would pick up the scent again, somewhere else. He knew it was a long shot. With no way of knowing which carriage was at the corner, it would be blind luck if they found another scent trail or a witness who knew something about the ring. Jimmy glumly looked around. His mission seemed hopeless. He prayed that Emma was faring better.

Chapter 7: Emma at the Yard

Emma loved Scotland Yard. She loved the contrast of the building's white Portland stone with its red brick walls. She loved the excitement of constables, sergeants, and inspectors running about, working on cases, interviewing witnesses, and locking up criminals. She loved the energy of a police force working to make London safe.

Since she arrived at the Yard with Inspector Lestrade, Emma had been hard at work. She was taking notes, conducting research, and interviewing Violet Vampire witnesses. As each person told their vampire tale, Emma was careful to write down all the facts and even to question the witnesses, sometimes on what appeared the most trifling matters. Sherlock Holmes had taught Emma that many cases are solved on the smallest of details.

"It was the size of a bus, that Violet Vampire. Its whole body glowed in a crimson red, like a bloody moon was coming after us," said one witness, a carpenter.

"It was the size of a humpback whale!" stated a different witness, a seamstress. "I've never seen anything like it. Probably comes from Mars."

Emma tried not to chuckle. She knew that these stories were exaggerated, and she would have to figure out which parts were true and which parts false.

"Did you notice a breeze?" Emma asked them. "Any flapping noise from the vampire's wings?"

Patiently, Emma wrote down all of their answers. After interviewing five witnesses, she noticed a pattern to their responses. Emma then pored over all of the news articles and notes from previous Violet Vampire sightings. She analyzed the data, and she kept adding to her notes. With all of the evidence before her, Emma deduced a solution to the Violet Vampire mystery.

"It's a fake!" she declared, bursting into Inspector Lestrade's office.

"What is?" asked Lestrade. He was sipping Earl Grey tea and sitting back in his office chair. On the desk before him he had notes from his own research. It had detailed sketches of the Violet Vampire as well as pictures of the Yeti, the Loch Ness Monster, and a strange metal block that appeared to be floating in the sky.

"The Violet Vampire. It isn't real. At least, it is not an animal," proudly declared Emma. She held up her notes for Lestrade to see. "My evidence is all here."

"Tut-tut, my dear," Lestrade smugly replied. He put down his tea cup and motioned with his left hand towards the pictures and notes on his own desk. "I too have been conducting my research, and as you can see, the Violet Vampire is very much a real creature, though it appears I was completely incorrect as to its origins."

"Origins?" Emma puzzled.

"Yes," explained Lestrade. "I was certain that the creature was some long lost ancestor of modern man. Perhaps it fit Mr. Darwin's theory of evolution. But after concluding my interviews today, I am convinced that the Vampire is none other than a creature from another planet!"

Emma's eyes widened in shock, and she then started coughing loudly. She let out long, hacking noises that echoed throughout the office. Emma didn't really have a cough. She was covering up, so she didn't burst out laughing.

"Are you alright, my dear? Would you like some water?" asked Lestrade.

"I'll...be...okay," Emma choked. She was trying her best to hide her smirk. "Please...tell me about your theory," she added, after regaining her composure.

"Several of the witnesses told me the vampire looked like something not from this world. One witness, a Mr. Baker, told me that the vampire said a word that sounded like Mars when it flew over his head. I did some research, as you can see from my pictures, and there have been reports of mysterious lights in the sky during sightings of the Loch Ness monster, the Yeti, and even the Violet Vampire. This leads us to the only obvious conclusion, that the creature is working with the other monsters, and they are all from another planet, maybe even the Moon!"

Emma was going to correct the Inspector and let him know that the Moon is not a planet, but she didn't want to make him upset. Lestrade had made a huge mistake that Sherlock Holmes always told Emma and Jimmy never to do. Inspector Lestrade had made the facts fit his theory instead of basing a theory off of the facts.

"Now," Lestrade continued, "what we need to do is to capture this alien and discover what it wants on Earth. What if it is the first part of an invasion?" Lestrade pondered. "We have to be delicate in this situation. We don't want a war of the worlds on our hands. Say, where are you going?"

Emma had gathered up all of her notes and was slowly walking towards the door. "Inspector Lestrade, thank you for letting me interview those witnesses. I have to go check up on my brother. Please let me know your plan for apprehending the vampire." Emma waved goodbye and quickly stepped out of the office. She wanted to add that she found the inspector's theory utterly ridiculous. No matter. She was going to bring her evidence and theory to someone who would listen, someone who could help her apprehend the Violet Vampire. Emma was going straight to

221B Baker Street, straight to Sherlock Holmes!

Chapter 8: An Unlikely Witness

Jimmy was at a loss. After traveling up and down the Strand for an hour, he had found no leads. Toby had sniffed over every square inch of the street, and he found no new traces of Mrs. MacDougall's ring.

After wandering up and down the Strand for the tenth time, Jimmy got an idea. He and Toby were standing in front of the Adelphi Theatre. The sign on the marquee said, *Sherlock Holmes and the Speckled Band*. There was a separate notice on a billboard in front of the entryway that said, "Due to an unexpected circumstance, the play entitled *Sherlock Holmes and the Speckled Band* has been delayed for one week. Tickets will be honored at the event's premiere. For more information, please see the **concierge**[9]."

---

[9] **Fun Fact:** A concierge is another name for a door-man. The concierge's duties are to monitor the comings and goings at hotels, restaurants, and theatres, to make certain all is in order.

Seeing the notice jogged Jimmy's memory. He thought back to the vampire's attack and remembered it had leaped off of the theatre's roof.

"Toby," Jimmy told the grey and frumpy dog, "if we can get up to that roof, you can get the scent of the vampire. Maybe we can find out where that vampire came from."

The boy and his dog approached the elegant oak and glass door of the theatre. Jimmy gave a quick rap-rap-rapping of the knocker and waited. A moment later, a well-dressed gentleman arrived at the door. He was standing perfectly stiff; his navy blue suit coat and collared shirt appeared to have not a wrinkle or speck of dust on them. His black hair was slicked back and held perfectly. Not one loose hair was out of place. "Yes," the concierge said in a deep, long, drawled out way, so it sounded like, "Yeeeeessss."

"Hello, sir, my name is Jimmy MacDougall of The Baker Street Youth Detectives. I work with Sherlock Holmes."

The concierge did not flinch or smile. He simply asked, "Is there something which I may do for you?"

"Yes, sir. I believe the Violet Vampire  leaped from the roof of the Adelphi Theatre last night. If I could take my dog, that is, Sherlock Holmes' dog, up there, we may be able to get the vampire's scent," Jimmy said excitedly.

The doorman lowered his eyes at the scruffy dog sitting next to Jimmy. Toby looked up at the concierge, tilted his head, and gave a soft whimper. Jimmy thought Toby looked like he was trying his best to be extra cute. The doorman screwed his face up into a look of absolute disgust. "This...thing," the doorman sneered, "cannot be allowed on the premises. We have a strict policy against dogs in our theatre. If you would like to return without your canine, perhaps we could accommodate you. Until then, good day!" And with that, the concierge slammed the door in Jimmy's face.

"I can't believe it." Jimmy was stunned. Toby gave the boy a reassuring lick on his right hand. "Thanks, Toby," Jimmy said and let out a long sigh. "I don't know what to do next."

"I might be able t' help yer," came a cockney voice from across the street. Jimmy turned to see a blind beggar quickly approaching him. It was the same beggar he had noticed when speaking to the bus driver. "I was there when the vampire attacked. Scary fellow, that one."

"But you can't see," Jimmy said matter-of-factly.

"No sir, I can't, not wif these," he said, and with both his pointer fingers motioned to his eyes. "But I can wif these," and he then pointed to his ears. "I hear things others can't and notice things others don't. Sometimes not having me eyes makes me more valuable, if yer gets my meanin."

Jimmy didn't get his meaning until the beggar shoved his tin cup right under Jimmy's nose. Jimmy thought for a second, then took a shilling out of his breast pocket, and tossed it into the beggar's cup.

"Oh, bless yer, lad. Yer see, last night I was standing on the corner as I usually do, when that vampire came flying down t' the street. Most footsteps I heard were running away from the vampire. But there were a few I heard heading in the opposite direction, walking towards the vampire. I was scared and confused, like everyone else. I didn't know what t' do nor where t' go. Then I noticed that the footstep I had heard approaching me had disappeared."

"Maybe they were just confused like you, sir," Jimmy suggested. "There were a lot of people running around terrified last night."

"Aye, there were, lad. But these footsteps weren't running. They were walking slowly, and when I noticed I didn't hear those footsteps anymore, I found that my tin cup was empty. All my money was gone, and I swear t' yer that

I didn't drop a single coin onto the pavement that night."

"You were robbed!" Jimmy blurted. "Of course, why didn't I see it?"

Jimmy tossed another shilling into the beggar's cup. He thanked the man for his information, and while the blind man was calling his blessings to the boy, Jimmy and Toby raced back to the end of the Strand, where Steven and Bess were waiting.

"Any luck?" Steven asked, hopefully.

"I think so, Steven! I think so!" he called to the driver. Jimmy and Toby hopped into the hansom. "To 221B Baker Street," he called to Steven, "and hurry!" The carriage started with a lurching jolt, and they were off.

Jimmy had to see Sherlock Holmes. He had to check his theory about the Violet Vampire. Jimmy couldn't believe he got his lead from a blind beggar. He was fortunate that the man had spoken to him. Jimmy thought of the man's face, his pale skin, dark glasses, and reddish hair. Why did the man seem familiar to Jimmy? Had he seen him before? It didn't matter, not really. With the help of Sherlock Holmes, Jimmy and his sister would solve the mystery of the Violet Vampire.

Chapter 9: Sherlock Holmes Joins the Case

Emma and Jimmy nearly collided with each other as their carriages dropped them in front of 221B Baker Street. The twins were bursting with excitement and couldn't contain it. "I have so much to tell you," both Jimmy and Emma said at the same time. Then they started talking over each other, Jimmy describing the thieves, and Emma explaining her Violet Vampire discoveries. They continued talking over each other and building in excitement 'til they both exploded in fits of laughter.

"Wow!" Emma called out through thick guffaws. "I guess we've both had productive days."

"We sure have, and I can see you wanted to tell Sherlock Holmes about your discoveries as well. So...let's head for Holmes," Jimmy said, waving to Sherlock's door.

"Head for Holmes," Emma said, emphasizing the pun Jimmy had said without realizing it, and they both ended up in a fit of giggles. After they regained their composure, the MacDougalls scampered over to 221B Baker Street, and hammered on the door.

With a sharp click, the door was opened by kindly old Mrs. Hudson. She was Mr. Holmes's landlord. She owned 221B Baker Street and rented rooms to Sherlock Holmes and Dr. Watson. "Well, well, well, if it isn't Jimmy and Emma MacDougall, and with Toby, the canine sleuth. I can tell from the looks on your faces that you're here to see Mr. Holmes."

"Yes, Mrs. Hudson," both twins said with elation.

"We have important information about the Violet Vampire!" Jimmy exploded. He couldn't hold back his excitement.

Mrs. Hudson gave a smile like a sunrise. She loved the twins and was good friends with their parents, especially Mrs. MacDougall. "Mr. Holmes will be delighted to see you children. He hasn't had much luck on his own case."

Emma, Jimmy, and Toby ascended the stairs to Sherlock Holmes's room. They had to use their strong willpower to keep from bounding up the steps. Emma and Jimmy knew Sherlock was deep in thought because they could hear him playing his violin, beautifully performing Beethoven for no one but his mind. This is what Sherlock called entering his mind palace. His brain analyzed data and deduced conclusions while his hands moved the violin bow and strings. Many horrible crimes had been solved by Sherlock Holmes playing Beethoven, Mozart, and Brahms.

Although he gave Mrs. Hudson strict instructions not to interrupt him when he was performing, the great detective was elated when he saw the twins enter his sitting room.

"It is truly a joyful occasion when you two grace me with your presence," the great detective told the twins. "I have once again been eluded by the Peterson gang, so it gives me pleasure to know you have made headway on your vampire case. Please sit down and tell me what you have learned."

    The twins sat down on a soft gray sofa. Emma began with her discoveries at Scotland Yard. "Every witness I interviewed, no matter how crazy their story, all said that the vampire's wings did not make sound. Most reported that the wings did not flap. They also said that the wind was supporting the vampire."

"They said the wind was supporting the vampire?" Sherlock asked with a raised eyebrow.

"Sorry Mr. Holmes," Emma apologized. "I should have said I deduced it. They all reported the vampire moving in the same direction of the wind. If the wind was blowing in a northwesterly direction then the vampire was also flying in that direction."

"Ahhh…" Sherlock Holmes said. He put away his violin, and then sat with his hands before his face, palms folded together, catching every last detail of Emma's story. "And you, James. What did you discover?"

Jimmy told Emma and Sherlock Holmes about his adventure with Toby, how the dog lost the scent at the end of the Strand, and the blind man's story of being robbed.

"I believe this means there are a gang of robbers working with the Violet Vampire. Whenever he attacks, the robbers pickpocket people in the confusion. This is what happened to Mom's ring. She didn't lose it; it was stolen," Jimmy concluded.

"Fascinating, Jimmy," Sherlock said, "but you are perhaps jumping to conclusions. We must have more information to make such a deduction."

"Actually," Emma answered, "when I interviewed the Violet Vampire witnesses, some did say they lost their wallets in the confusion. One even lost her wedding ring. I thought they were correct, but with what Jimmy says, it makes sense that the gang is working with the vampire."

"Very good," Sherlock Holmes nodded his head towards the twins. "Now, you still are not done yet. With all of the evidence you have before you, what is the Violet Vampire?"

As the twins began discussing their ideas, Sherlock Holmes watched with a serious expression on his face. He was impressed at how the twins could analyze data and draw conclusions, often coming to the correct answer. Very few people on Earth had this ability; even

Dr. Watson could come to completely wrong conclusions when analyzing the same data as Sherlock Holmes or the MacDougall twins. These children were special and Holmes saw them as equals.

"I believe we have figured it out," Emma stated. "We can't know for certain until we apprehend the flyer, but the Violet Vampire is a glider device."

"A glider device?" Holmes pressed.

"Yes," continued Jimmy. "Since George Cayley began glider flights in 1849, the devices have become more and more sophisticated. Gliders are aircrafts which allow people to fly along air currents. Glider wings don't flap, and they don't require engines like airships. Someone following the designs of **Otto**

Lilienthal[10] could have made a flying device that works like the Violet Vampire."

"The person using the Violet Vampire glider leaps off of a building, soars along air currents, and scares the people in the street below it," continued Emma. "The vampire's gang then go to work, robbing the people who flee from the flying creature. By the time the vampire lands, all the witnesses have panicked and run away, terrified of the monster. The person in the vampire glider probably lands in an alley, takes his suit off, and then gets away with his gang in a carriage."

---

[10] **Fun Fact:** Otto Lilienthal was considered the Glider King. His glider

devices led people to realize other flying devices, such as helicopters and airplanes, were possible.

"It certainly makes more sense than Inspector Lestrade's alien from the moon theory," Jimmy added jokingly.

"Very well done, twins. You always make me proud," stated Sherlock Holmes. "Now, it is time for me to pay a visit to Inspector Lestrade."

"Mr. Holmes, I don't think even you can convince Inspector Lestrade that the Violet Vampire is not real," explained Emma.

Sherlock Holmes stood from his chair and grabbed his hat and jacket. "On the contrary, Emma. I want Inspector Lestrade to continue believing his outlandish theory. That is how we will get the misguided inspector to catch the Violet Vampire."

Chapter 10: The Violet Vampire Attacks

The Violet Vampire peered over the edge of his rooftop perch to see a growing crowd of spectators lining Baker Street. It was another perfect night for an attack. The wind howled from a strong breeze that the vampire knew would give sufficient support for its assault. This would be the final attack before the great showing next week. Then the world would know the truth of the Violet Vampire's genius.

The creature chuckled while it heard the first calls of excitement from the crowd below. A rumor had been announced in the news that the gold anointing spoon, the oldest piece of the crown jewels, would be moved from the Tower of London to a new, special display located in the Royal Botanic Gardens. The spoon would be brought by two royal guards in an open **phaeton carriage**[11]. They would travel down Baker Street, then cross over on The Outer Circle, and finally end up in the Inner Circle of the Royal Botanic Gardens. That was the supposed plan, and the Violet Vampire did not believe a word of it. Rumors and hoaxes were constantly printed in the news, and the Royal Family would never risk having their gold anointing spoon get stolen.

With news reporters mixed in the crowd of onlookers, it was a perfect opportunity for the

---

[11] **Fun Fact:** A phaeton carriage is a sporty four-wheeled coach drawn by one or two horses.

Violet Vampire to strike. It would soar down towards the crowd. When the crowd saw its massive black form, they would scream and flee. The next day the vampire would be on the front page of the newspapers one last time. It would wait three days, then the creature would make its grand entrance, leaping down from the top of Big Ben, and announcing itself to the world.

"It's here! It's here!" came a cry from the street below, as the royal carriage came into view. The Violet Vampire was stunned. It hadn't believed the rumors, but there was the royal carriage. Calls of excitement came from the onlookers. Some clapped, others cheered. The vampire saw that the coach was painted an elegant blue and black, royal colors. There was a single brown Cleveland Bay pulling the four wheeled carriage. The two coachmen, dressed in the traditional red and gold uniform, paused and waved at the crowd.

As shocked as the vampire was, it knew the timing was perfect for an attack. The Violet

Vampire took a few steps back, then charged. The monster leaped off the building rooftop and soared into the air. The calls and cheers of excitement turned to screams of fear as the crowd of people saw the vampire above them. The monster swooped down towards an elderly man who was trying his best to run away. The vampire grabbed the man in his claws and lifted him off the ground. The man screeched and cried. The vampire then tossed him down to the street below. Fortunately, the man landed on an old mattress someone had abandoned on the sidewalk.

With a shift of its wings, the creature elevated itself up and spied a couple standing in the center of the street in absolute horror. They were frozen with fear. Using its claws, the vampire flew just above their heads then ripped the bonnet from the woman's head, and the bowler from the gentleman. The monster tore the hats to pieces and let the shredded bits of fabric rain down on the street below.

At last, the Violet Vampire found itself at the Royal Coach. The two coachmen were trembling in their seats, and the horse, surprisingly, was standing still. Perhaps the horse was too scared to make a move. The vampire would change that. It planned on gliding just over the horse, then giving the animal a smack to send it wildly running off. That would surely make the newspapers!

The vampire could see the sleek, brown hair of the horse. Clearly, the Cleveland Bay was well taken care of at the Royal Mews. The vampire was over the animal now, it reached out with its left hand, claws extended, ready to slap the animal. Suddenly the vampire saw a patterned wall before it, like it was flying into several linked chains. The creature lurched, then switched gears, trying to pull up quickly. It was too late. With a solid thud, the Violet Vampire slammed into the wall, only to realize that it was a net. The net had been hidden behind the royal carriage, and now the vampire was caught. It struggled, but its wings were folded up, and the Violet Vampire came crashing to the street below.

"We have him! We have him!" cried a man from the street. The Violet Vampire could see it was an inspector, and next to him were a young girl and a mangy dog. The vampire fought hard against the ropes. It never thought anyone would try and catch it, never in a million years. The two coach drivers had leapt off the phaeton and were now standing beside the vampire's crumpled form. It could see that one of the coachmen was just a mere boy dressed up to look like an older man. The other one, with his hooked nose and piercing vulture eyes, looked very familiar. But... The vampire shuddered when it realized where it had seen a picture of a man with a similar high forehead and lanky body before. This coachman was none other than the famous Sherlock Holmes.

"Inspector Lestrade," the great detective said, "I think it is fitting for you to have the honor to be the first man to see the true face of the Violet Vampire."

Emma, Toby, several constables, and the inspector had now joined the detective and Jimmy, surrounding the Violet Vampire.

"What do you mean by true face?" asked Inspector Lestrade. "This is an alien from another world. This situation now calls for delicate diplomacy."

"Very well, then," gleefully stated Sherlock Holmes. "I invite you to meet your supposed man from outer space." And with that

last word, Sherlock Holmes removed the Violet
Vampire's head.

Chapter 11: The Tale of the Violet Vampire

Jimmy gasped. Emma gasped. Inspector Lestrade and the police officers gasped. Sherlock Holmes had a knowing look of satisfaction upon his face as he held the head of the Violet Vampire in his hands. All eyes were on the form of the Violet Vampire.

The vampire was no more than a suit of lightweight armor with sturdy gargoyle wings. The wings, now folded and caught in the net, must have had a twenty foot wingspan when fully spread apart.

The gasp from the audience came not from the discovery of the flying machine, but from the machine's pilot, for inside the vampire suit was not a burly, sneering villain, but a young girl, slightly older than Emma.

The girl had long, jet black hair that was put up in a bun, much like Mrs. MacDougall's hair. She had a thin, gaunt face, sparkling jade eyes, and an elongated nose she held up at a slight tilt. Her mouth was pursed in a thin frown, and with an air of superiority, she glared at the small crowd gathered before her.

"You sir," she said, addressing Sherlock in a haughty tone, "have ruined my awe-inspiring debut. I was to make a grand entrance before Buckingham Palace next Wednesday. Now, I suppose, I must settle for my unmasking before this minuscule crowd. Still, with Sherlock Holmes in the audience, I know I shall make the morning editions."

The crowd was flabbergasted at this young lady's attitude of defiance. Everyone sputtered at the same time.

"I can't believe you!" stammered Jimmy.

"So rude!" snapped Emma.

"The idea that a girl with such poor manners..." started one constable.

"...Could be behind the Violet Vampire attacks!" finished another.

"You, my dear, are under arrest," began Lestrade," for several most heinous crimes: disturbing the peace, assault, causing untold damage, and possibly most distressing of all, impersonating an interplanetary ambassador!"

"Perhaps," the great detective said calmly, "we should hear why this young lady has caused so much mayhem."

"I have done no such thing," the girl sneered at the group. "Instead of arresting me, you should be praising me. I have done no more than prove myself a capable and worthy inventor, but because I was not a man of significant means, my greatness has been largely ignored, until now."

The girl's obstinacy and snobbish attitude had now angered the police. Inspector Lestrade, red in the face and clutching his fists, snapped, "I have heard just about enough from you!"

He would have hauled the girl away if not for Sherlock Holmes raising his right index finger to his lips, urging Lestrade to remain silent.

"Let this... child... finish her tale," Sherlock Holmes said, purposely making the word *child* sound dismissive of the girl.

"Oh, a mere child, am I?" raged the girl who was the Violet Vampire. "My true name is Permelia Jenkins, and like you two," she said pointing to the MacDougall twins, "I was not satisfied with my lot in life. Being a girl, I was forced to stay in school all day learning how to sit correctly, hold a fork, and tend to children. What a waste for a brain such as mine!

"I found myself often daydreaming and watching the birds out the window, how free they were fluttering through the air. As I was walking with a book of Shakespeare balanced upon my head to show good poise and steadiness, I came upon a most brilliant idea. I would design a device that would allow a person such as myself to take to the air like the falcons and jays."

"So you designed the vampire suit, and no one took you seriously," surmised Sherlock Holmes.

"Precisely," admitted Permelia. "I shared the designs with the headmistress, who merely laughed and tossed them into the fire. I redrew my plans and concealed them in my boarding room, anxiously awaiting a visit from my parents. Instead of the praise I expected from them, they merely scorned at my work. My mother told me I was such a disappointment and would never find a good husband if I kept up this work. Bah! I am a mere twelve years old and have no interest in husbands."

"How did you manage to build the vampire suit if no one took you seriously?" asked Emma sympathetically. She knew what it meant to be dismissed simply because she was a girl.

"Luckily, fortune smiled upon me," explained Permelia. "A few months ago, my school was on a day out in London. While the girls were focusing on walking upright and holding their parasols correctly, I clutched my plans for my flying device and managed to sneak away into the city crowds.

"I took **the Underground**[12] to various inventors throughout London. Most refused to see me. Those that did, refused to even look at my work. The minute an engineer saw who was in his waiting room, his face would drop, and I would be shown the door. My hopes were disappearing as quickly as the setting sun. I had spent all day searching for someone to

---

[12] **Fun Fact:** The Underground or Tube is the name of the London subway system. Originally, the Underground consisted of horse drawn carriages below the city. By 1897, the Underground was made up of trains, making it the first underground railway.

acknowledge that my flying machine plans were sound, yet no one even studied them. Crestfallen, I was about to head home, when I finally found an engineer interested in my blueprints. I was thrilled when Mr. Bruce Partington not only agreed to see me, he looked over the plans, and marveled at their brilliance."

Emma noticed a slight look of surprise cross Sherlock Holmes's face at the mention of the name Bruce Partington. She wondered if the detective was going to interrupt Permelia, but his expression returned to normal, and he allowed the girl to continue her tale.

"Mr. Partington returned me to my school. We came up with a story of how I was lost in the city, and he kindly gave me a ride home. My headmistress believed his every word. Before he left, Mr. Partington and I devised an ingenious plan. He would get a workshop near the school, and each night, I would sneak away and work on the flying device.

"Within a week, we were constructing the glider. Mr. Partington wanted to make sure that I received proper credit for my invention. He and I concocted the idea of a vampire attacking London. Once everyone followed the vampire, there was no way anyone could take away my credit when I finally revealed myself as the inventor of the flying monster."

"But why did you make the vampire violet?" Jimmy interrupted.

"I was getting to that part," snapped Permelia. "We wanted people to be able to see the vampire, but we didn't want it bright or people would see where I landed, and my costume would be revealed too early.

"We settled on a violet paint. We also added reflective glass to the eyes, so that the streetlight would reflect in them, and make it appear like the eyes were glowing.

"As you know," Permelia said directly to Sherlock Holmes, "the plan worked perfectly. Each time I leaped from a rooftop, I made the papers, and more and more people believed in the Violet Vampire. Now the world will know the brilliance of Permelia Jenkins!"

Inspector Lestrade was not impressed. "Young lady, you still have not explained about your part in all of the robberies."

To everyone's surprise, Permelia looked genuinely confused. "Robberies? What robberies?" she asked, and wondered if Inspector Lestrade was daffy.

Before Lestrade could answer, a constable raced up the street on a galloping horse. "Inspector Lestrade! Inspector Lestrade!" the officer called. "It's the Bank of England! It's just been robbed!!"

Chapter 12: Everyone Makes Mistakes, Even Sherlock Holmes

Inspector Lestrade, Sherlock Holmes, the MacDougall Twins, and the rest of the crowd stood around the newly arrived constable, and listened to the details of the bank robbery.

"They stole over a million pounds!" The constable explained about the robbery. "They knocked out the guard and broke into the bank's vault."

"Where were our officers?" asked Lestrade.

"Right here," answered Sherlock Holmes, gesturing to the extra officers with the Violet Vampire. "The robbers knew extra police would be needed to catch the vampire. It was a perfect night to rob the bank."

"But how did they know about the Violet Vampire?" asked Jimmy.

"They knew because they tricked me," admitted Permelia glumly. "I'll bet that Bruce Partington was one of the robbers."

"Yes," admitted Holmes, "but his real name is not Bruce Partington." The detective paused for a moment and reflected on the robbery. "Let us return to 221B. Mrs. Hudson will prepare some food. It will give me time to work through the details of what transpired."

The officers said their goodbyes. They were off to the Bank of England to look for clues. Lestrade stayed to keep watch over Permelia.

He wasn't sure if she was innocent. He didn't want her to try and escape.

They all went to 221B Baker Street and climbed the stairs to Sherlock Holmes's sitting room. Mrs. Hudson brought them tea and biscuits. While they were snacking, Dr. Watson, and the MacDougall parents arrived at 221B Baker Street. They had been stuck in traffic and missed the unveiling of the Violet Vampire.

"I'm just glad you two are safe," Mrs. MacDougall said to the twins. Then she said to Permelia, "I am impressed by your invention, young lady."

"I'd be more impressed if it were a real vampire," grumbled Mr. MacDougall. He was disappointed there was no monster.

"Thank you for your compliment, Mrs. MacDougall. I fear now, because of my ignorance, the flying device will now only be known as a work of evil. Everyone will always think of the Violet Vampire when they hear my name. No one will ever hire me. I will never be an inventor," Permelia lamented.

"I feel the same way," complained Emma. "I can't believe I never saw a connection between the vampire and a larger robbery plot. If I keep making mistakes, I'll never be a detective, certainly not a great one like Sherlock Holmes."

"That goes for me too, Emma," Jimmy stated gloomily. He had been the detective working on the missing diamond ring. He felt like he had let everyone down. He should have figured out that the robbery was more than just pickpockets working on the street.

"You three are being much too hard on yourselves," Sherlock Holmes responded to Permelia and the twins.

"No disrespect, sir," Emma answered, "but you *are* Sherlock Holmes. You don't make mistakes."

"I don't make mistakes?" Holmes asked with a slight chuckle in his voice. For the first time that night, a smile appeared upon Sherlock's visage. The detective looked over at Dr. Watson, who now had a grin on his face and a twinkle in his eye.

"Let me tell you that not all of my cases are written down by Dr. Watson. There are several cases from my early years as a detective that I never solved. There are times when I have made foolish errors. Just this year, I made a mistake which proved almost fatal. I had tested a chemical substance I discovered at a crime scene. I put the mixture in a fire, and it released a deadly gas. If Dr. Watson hadn't been in the room with me, I might have died. He pushed me out of the room and saved my life."

Mr. Holmes walked over to Dr. Watson and put his left arm over his shoulder. He gave the doctor a pat on his back. "If it wasn't for Dr. Watson, my Boswell, I fear my career would have been short lived. The good doctor has saved my life on numerous occasions. I am lucky to have such a great friend.

"My point though, is that even with the best reasoning skills, you are still bound to make mistakes, even if you are Sherlock Holmes."

Permelia, Emma and Jimmy listened to the words of the great detective, and it did make them feel better. Knowing that even Sherlock Holmes makes mistakes allowed them to get past their gloom, and it gave them hope.

"Well," Permelia said to the twins, "the night is still young, and I'd like to get my hands on that Bruce Partington." Here, Permelia clenched her fists. She wanted revenge on the man who tricked her.

"Mr. Holmes, who is this Bruce Partington?" asked Emma.

Sherlock Holmes went to a desk, opened the top drawer, and removed a photograph. He showed the picture to Permelia. She saw the image of a balding middle aged man with a high forehead. "Why, yes, that is Mr. Partington," Permelia admitted. "But why do you have a picture of him?"

"Just a minute," Jimmy said. "I know that face. That's the blind beggar who told me about the robbers. He set me up!"

"Yes, he did," admitted Sherlock. "This man is none other than Jeb Peterson of the Peterson gang."

"Bruce Partington is one of his fake names," Dr. Watson said, continuing Sherlock Holmes's explanation. "Mr. Holmes worked on a case where secret documents, known as the **Bruce-Partington**[13] plans, were put on the black market. They were plans for a super submarine. If villains built the submarine, they could have caused untold damage to England and the world. Jeb Peterson must have been one of the criminals trying to buy the plans. He liked the name Bruce-Partington and added it as one of his identities."

---

[13] **Fun Fact:** "The Adventure of the Bruce-Partington Plans," is one of the original Sherlock Holmes stories. Because Bruce-Partington is hyphenated, it means the plans were named after two people, Mr. Bruce and Mr. Partington. Jeb Peterson took the two names and combined them to make the identity of Bruce Partington.

"Did you ever find the secret documents?" asked Mr. MacDougall.

Dr. Watson's face lit up. "Oh yes, it was a wonderful case. I'll have to write that tale one day."

"But how will we solve this mystery?" Emma wondered aloud. "How will we catch the Violet Vampire? We now have no leads, no witnesses at the bank robbery, not even a loose thread."

"Wait a minute!" screamed Jimmy, and he jumped out of his seat. "I've got it! I think I know how we can catch Jeb Peterson!"

Chapter 13: The Vampire's Revenge

Jeb Peterson and his gang sat around an oak table in their hideout at the edge of London. The gang leader and his cronies were each having a pint of ale. They were taking a break before dividing up their stolen loot.

"A toast," called out Fats Larson, an eye-patched member of the gang who looked like a pirate from a Robert Louis Stevenson novel. "A toast to Jeb Peterson, the man who out-thunk Sherlock Holmes!"

""Hear, Hear!!" came a cheer from everyone at the table.

"Gentlemen," Mr. Peterson called to them after everyone had taken a swig of their drink. "I could not have done it without you. Can you see poor Permelia now? I'm sure that smart-mouthed brat is shocked to find herself under arrest. The police will pin all of the robberies on her, and Sherlock Holmes will never connect us to the Violet Vampire. That dumb detective will keep running in circles. Soon, we'll be in Dublin, and we'll rob the Bank of Ireland."

Another, "Hear, Hear!" came from the table.

"Then," Peterson continued. "We'll go to America and rob the Boston Museum of Fine Arts. Then, we'll sail across the seas and finally go to Australia!"

"What'll we do there, boss?" asked Willey Pike, the notorious gunman.

"Why, we'll get even more men for our gang. Australians are known to be a wild bunch. From there, who knows, maybe we'll even rob the Louvre in Paris of all its famous paintings. Gentlemen, there is no stopping us now!"

The robbers all clapped and shouted. They drank their ale and burst into song. They would have continued on like that until dawn if it wasn't for a thunderous bang they heard at the front door. It sounded as if a meteorite had landed right at their doorstep.

"What was that?" growled Fats Larson. The gang members all took out their knives and pistols. Then, the group slowly approached the door.

"It could be the cops," Jeb said. He had his Webley pistol in his left hand as he slowly lifted the front door latch with his right. Jeb pushed the door open a crack and peered outside. All he saw was the light of the full moon and heard the chirping of insects.

"I guess it's nothing," Jeb started to say when **Bam!** The front door was torn off its hinges. Jeb Peterson fell back into his gang members, and they all tumbled to the floor. When they turned to look to the doorway, the gang members gasped, cried, and trembled. For there in the doorway, looming above them, was the Violet Vampire.

But it wasn't the Violet Vampire that they all knew, not the one that flew from rooftops and threatened London. This Violet Vampire was much bigger. Its arms were bulkier. Its wings flapped. Large purple spikes covered its back.

"Jeb Peterson," the Violet Vampire's voice boomed. "You dared to mimic one of my kind by building a vampire device. Now, you shall feel the full fury of the real Violet Vampire!"

The gang members screamed and fled to the back door entrance, stepping on each other's feet, and stumbling over each other. They all wanted to get as far away from the Violet Vampire as possible.

Not Jeb Peterson, though. As he tried to sprint away, the vampire grabbed his shirt collar and dragged him back outside. When they were a few yards from the house, the vampire said, "You were a fool to pretend to be a vampire. And I will make sure you never do it again!"

"Please," Jeb whimpered and pleaded. The vampire, still clutching the gun man, lifted the man into the air, his feet dangling six inches above the ground. "Puh-please. I didn't know that you was real. No one thought there was real vampires. None of my gang did. Honest, we didn't. I'll do anything to make this right."

"Do I look real to you now?" the Vampire bellowed and threw Jeb Peterson into the air. His body came crashing down onto the ground.

"Oww," Jeb Peterson howled. He looked up to see the vampire, with its claws extended, fast approaching. "Please," Jeb called to the Vampire. "Please...it wasn't my idea. It was a girl. Yes, that's it. Her name was Permelia Jenkins. She's the one who dressed up as a vampire. She's the one you want."

The vampire glared down at Jeb and snarled. "You expect me to believe that a little girl could imitate one of my kind. That girl would have to be a genius, someone much smarter than you."

"Oh, she was," Jeb stammered, hoping the vampire would leave him alone and go after Permelia. "She was smart. She was cunning. I wasn't anywhere near as intelligent as her."

"Hmmm..." the vampire pondered. "I'll go after this brilliant Permelia Jenkins, after I deal with you!!"

"No!" begged Jeb Peterson. He had his hands folded together, praying for his life. "I will do anything if you let me go. Anything. I don't wanna die!"

"Anything?" asked the vampire. "Will you confess to your crimes?"

"Yes, I'll admit I robbed the Bank of London. You can have all the money we took. It's all inside. We didn't have a chance to spend any of it. Please, just don't hurt me."

Jeb expected to feel the claw of the vampire clutch him and bring him up to the monster's mouth. He expected to feel the creature's hot breath upon him as its fangs bit into him. Jeb expected that this was his end. He cowered and waited for the vampire to pounce. Instead, he was perplexed as he heard roars of laughter all around him.

Chapter 14: How They Solved It

"What is the meaning of this?!?" growled Jeb Peterson. The Violet Vampire still loomed in front of him. Two constables had lifted Mr. Peterson off of the ground and bound his hands. Off to the side of the vampire was the boy Jeb saw in front of the Adelphi Theatre with his dog, Sherlock Holmes, Inspector Lestrade, and Dr. Watson. There were two other adults behind the vampire as well. Jeb guessed they were the boy's parents.

"Unhand me, you brutes!" Jeb called out to the police officers. "I am the victim here. That thing over there was ready to kill me. You should arrest that monster!"

"Monster?" asked the Violet Vampire, although this time it did not have a threatening voice. This time the vampire spoke in a voice Jeb knew all too well. This time the voice was that of Permelia Jenkins. "I believe you called me a genius. I'm the one who outsmarted you."

Jeb was surprised to hear a second voice come from the Violet Vampire. "Hey, I think we helped a lot, Permelia," came a different girl's voice.

Mr. and Mrs. MacDougall took the head off of the Violet Vampire, revealing Emma MacDougall at the top of the machine. They then opened the lower body, revealing Permelia Jenkins.

"Impossible," sputtered Jeb Peterson.

"Actually, quite elementary," responded Sherlock Holmes. "Permelia had been working on this second Violet Vampire prototype."

"That is correct," Permelia continued, interrupting the great detective. "As you can see, this is a much heavier device. I constructed it as a backup device in case anyone attempted to, how should I say, shoot me out of the sky. The front chest plate is a thick steel that would stop any bullet."

"And the arms," continued Emma, "are controlled by this pulley system." Emma showed the intricate controls for the arms and claws. "The balance of weight and pressure allowed the vampire to have astounding strength. It is how I ripped the door off of its hinges."

"I moved the legs, with these stilt devices," continued Permelia. She interrupted Emma to make sure she could finish the description. Permelia showed how she got the vampire to walk by moving her left and right leg with the stilts. "Lastly, I added the flapping wings for effect. We used internal ropes to move the wings up and down. Alas, this vampire was too heavy. I never could get it off of the ground, at least not by flying. I could do this."

Permelia made the vampire jump into the air. It came down hard, making a thunderous crash, shaking the house and making Dr. Watson teeter for a second. Sherlock Holmes made sure his good friend did not fall to the ground.

"So that's the big crash we heard outside. Still, you made a big mistake my dear. You caught me, but the rest of the Peterson gang is on the loose. They'll come after you," Jeb threatened. He glowered at Sherlock Holmes. "They'll get all of you! Even the supposed world's greatest detective."

"All your team will get is a good twenty years behind bars," came a voice from behind Jeb Peterson. It was Inspector Lestrade. He stepped out from inside the house. "As your team exited through the back door, my constabulary was there to arrest them all. Soon you will rejoin your gang, in prison."

"Bah!" snapped Peterson. "I'll get loose. You'll see. No prison can hold the likes of Jeb Peterson, and when I do, I'll make sure you all pay for what you've done here today."

"Empty threats do not become you, Jeb," Sherlock Holmes said dismissively. "You may take him away now, officers."

As the two police officers began hauling Jeb away, the criminal called out. "One more question. How did you find my hideout?"

"Actually, sir, that was because of me and Sherlock Holmes's most special agent," Jimmy said, and he pointed down to Toby, who smiled up at the boy. "When I saw you on the strand, and you were disguised as the blind beggar, I kept thinking there was something familiar about you. I couldn't place it until after you had robbed the Bank of England. Then, when we were all talking at 221B Baker Street, it dawned on me. The stitching of your front buttons. There is only one seamstress in

London who sews hexagonal patterns of thread to hold her buttons in place, and that is Sally, the seamstress. We went to see Sally. She remembered you. She said you still hadn't paid your bills, so she was holding some of your shirts until you did. We gave one of your shirts to Toby. That was all he needed to lead us straight to this hideout."

Toby gave a quick bark of approval.

"Now men, take him away," concluded Inspector Lestrade. Jeb continued cursing Sherlock Holmes, Permelia, and the MacDougalls as he was led off to a police wagon.

"Well, that wrapped up nicely," stated Dr. Watson proudly. "The MacDougall twins, once again, showed their worth and merit. Permelia's genius helped catch the crooks. Holmes helped put the pieces together, and Toby led us straight to the Peterson gang. Solving this case was an excellent example of teamwork."

"Aren't you forgetting something?" asked Inspector Lestrade.

"Ah, yes," muttered Dr. Watson. "I suppose you did help in some ways Lestrade. After your wild theories did not pan out, your officers did arrest the Peterson gang."

"That's not what I was referencing," Inspector Lestrade said with a sly grin. "When I was in the criminal's hideout and checking their stolen money, I found this." Inspector Lestrade held up the MacDougall family ring. "Mrs. MacDougall, I do believe this belongs to you." With that, Inspector Lestrade proudly walked up to Mr. MacDougall, handed him the ring, and he slid it onto his wife's finger.

"Oh Inspector Lestrade," Mrs. MacDougall stammered with tears in her eyes. "How can I ever thank you?"

"All in the line of duty, ma'am," Lestrade said proudly.

"Three cheers for Inspector Lestrade," called out Mr. MacDougall. Everyone cheered, except for Toby, who barked approvingly.

Jimmy stood next to Emma, now that she was free from the vampire suit. "Can you believe that the man who thought the Violet Vampire was from Mars found mom's ring?"

"With teamwork, Jimmy, everyone plays a part. Even Inspector Lestrade can save the day."

Chapter 15: A Night at the Adelphi Theatre

It had been a week since the arrest of the Peterson gang. Life had gone back to normal for the MacDougall Twins and Sherlock Holmes. Jimmy and Emma had been focusing on their studies. Holmes had not had a case, so he was focusing on his violin playing. Now, the group was back at the Adelphi Theatre for the debut of *Sherlock Holmes and The Speckled Band*.

Since the play had been delayed, Sherlock Holmes was able to get extra tickets. The great detective looked to the seats behind him. There sat Permelia Jenkins, her parents, and Mycroft Holmes, Sherlock's older brother. Mycroft worked for the British government. After the conclusion of the Violet Vampire Adventure, Sherlock had asked Mycroft to find an apprenticeship for Permelia. When Mycroft had seen Permelia's skills, he quickly found her an engineering apprenticeship. He also went to her parents and told them about her daughter's genius. Mycroft was able to get Permelia's parents to agree to keep her at home while she learned engineering. They now understood that their daughter had more talents than balancing books on her head.

Sitting in front of Sherlock Holmes was Inspector Lestrade and the other constables who helped arrest the Peterson gang. Lestrade was reading a pamphlet on strange airships seen over the American West. Holmes smiled as he saw Lestrade write down, "Are these airships from Mars? I'll have to investigate."

Sitting to Holmes's left was the MacDougall family. Mrs. MacDougall was proudly displaying her ring. In fact, she kept poking Mr. MacDougall with it to make sure he stayed awake. Jimmy and Emma were chatting between themselves. Sherlock was as proud of the twins as always. He knew that if he ever had to take a case that required him to travel, the twins would make sure London remained safe.

To Sherlock's right was Dr. Watson. He was excited to see what the Adelphi Theatre did with his story. He wanted to know how it would work as a play. Would they make it as scary as the original story?

"Watson," Holmes leaned over and whispered to his friend, "I have heard that the playwrights took some liberty with your tale."

"What do you mean by liberty?" asked the doctor. "Did they give me a bigger part?"

"They did, however..." started the great detective, but he had to be quiet as the lights went out and the show began.

On the stage, a square-jawed actor who was much more muscular than Sherlock Holmes walked into the light. "My name is Holmes," he said coolly. "Sherlock Holmes. Tonight I will solve a mystery like no other you've ever seen."

Suddenly, a huge crash was heard back stage. An actor, who was overweight and poorly dressed, stumbled onto the stage. His glasses were crooked, his hair was a mess, and his suspenders barely held up his pants. "I am Dr. Watson!" he called out proudly, then he tripped over his own two feet and fell head first into a bucket of water.

The audience roared. Mr. MacDougall almost fell out of his seat from laughing so hard. He turned to Dr. Watson and gave him a thumbs up. Watson was red in the face. "They turned me into a bumbling idiot," he snarled.

He expected Sherlock Holmes to come to his defense. Instead, the great detective was chuckling. He turned to Watson and said, "Now you know how I feel when you change some things about me in your stories, like having me target practice with a revolver indoors."

Watson grumbled, but he agreed sometimes he did bend the truth in his stories, and he also knew this was a fun night. He watched as the MacDougalls, the Jenkins, and the police laughed and applauded the wacky version of himself that appeared onstage. In the end, Dr. Watson found himself laughing too.

After all, a good story is a good story, no matter how strange it is in its telling.

Special Thanks

Derrick Belanger would like to thank all of the people who offered feedback and advice while he wrote this exceptional story: Harrison and Chris Cramer; Jennifer Viers; Karen Cohn, your advice, as always, was invaluable; Tracy Johnson; Greg Dufford; The Moriarty family (Pat, Stefanie, Bryn, and Cedar. But certainly not James.) The great David Marcum (or, perhaps, Jeb Peterson?); Steve Emecz; and, of course, Chuck and Claudia Davis, who still remain the world's two biggest kids. Without your valuable insights, he couldn't have made this delightful adventure.

The author would also like to thank Dr. Dan Andriacco, Griffin Garcon, Timothy Hillmer, Mike Hogan, Kieran Lyne, Jack McDevitt, Dean K. Miller, Eric Pellerin, Jennifer Petkus, Kristi Peterson Schoonover, Elizabeth Varadan, and K.M. Weiland for the positive reviews to his previous works; GC Rosenquist, Anita Golden, and Les "Dome" Rosenthal – paying it forward; Sir Arthur Conan Doyle for creating the world's greatest literary character; Dr. Watson's Neglected

Patients, his local Sherlockian posse; Scott Monty for the opportunity to write for *I Hear of Sherlock Everywhere*; his parents, Dennis and Ellen Belanger, and grandmother, Barbara Rousseau, for their support; Brian Belanger, the best big brother he could ask for; Traci Belanger, for letting Brian out to play; Abigail Gosselin, his wife, for not minding too much the time the writing took away from family and chores; and Rhea for not minding too much that her little sister also has a book dedicated to her.

Brian Belanger would like to thank all of his family and friends for understanding that he hasn't disappeared --- HE JUST NEEDS TO DRAW. Thanks for still being there when he emerges blinking from his cave with a new book in hand.

Author Derrick Belanger is the editor of the bestselling two volume anthology, *A Study in Terror: Sir Arthur Conan Doyle's Revolutionary Stories of Fear and the Supernatural*, which may be too scary for readers of this book. He also is the author of *The MacDougall Twins with Sherlock Holmes* series, and a contributor to the *I Hear of Sherlock* Everywhere blog. He is a middle school Language Arts teacher, and he loves young adult literature as well as anything and everything to do with Sherlock Holmes. Derrick lives in Broomfield, Colorado with his wife, Abigail Gosselin, and their two daughters, Rhea and Phoebe.

Illustrator Brian Belanger is the cover artist and a contributor to the bestselling two volume anthology *A Study in Terror: Sir Arthur Conan Doyle's Revolutionary Stories of Fear and the Supernatural*, as well as being the artist for *The MacDougall Twins with Sherlock Holmes* series. He has always loved to draw, laugh, dance and sing, but not always when other people are around. Brian lives in Manchester, New Hampshire with his wife Traci.

You can learn more about Derrick and Brian Belanger

By visiting our web site, **Belanger Books**, at: www.belangerbooks.com.

For those of you old enough to be on Social Media, you can find us

On Facebook at:

https://www.facebook.com/groups/Belangerbooks/

On Twitter at:

https://twitter.com/belangerbooks

And if you'd like to send us an email, send it to

belangerbooks@gmail.com

CPSIA information can be obtained at www.ICGtesting.com
Printed in the USA
BVOW08s0512010615

401960BV00007B/41/P

9 781780 927671